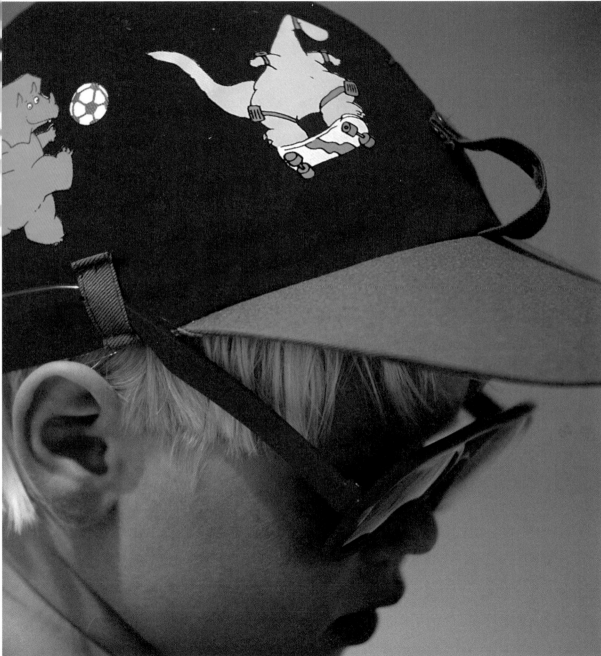

Until I saw the sea

A COLLECTION OF SEASHORE POEMS

Alison Shaw

HENRY HOLT
AND COMPANY
NEW YORK

Many thanks to Laura Godwin and Sue Dawson — A.S.

Permission for the use of the following is gratefully acknowledged:

Joanna Cole for "Driving to the Beach." Copyright © 1973 by Joanna Cole.

D.A.W. for "How to Swim." Copyright © 1993 by D.A.W.
Reprinted with his permission.

HarperCollins Publishers, Inc., for "Sitting in the Sand," from
Dogs & Dragons, Trees & Dreams by Karla Kuskin. Copyright © 1958 by Karla
Kuskin. Reprinted by permission of HarperCollins Publishers, Inc.

Nola Buck for "Seashore Recipe." Copyright © 1995 by Nola Buck.
Reprinted with her permission.

Little, Brown and Company, for "The Shell" from *One at a Time*
by David McCord. Copyright © 1952 by David McCord.
Reprinted by permission of Little, Brown and Company.

Myra Cohn Livingston for "Seaweed," from *Wide Awake and Other Poems*
by Myra Cohn Livingston. Copyright © 1959, renewed 1987 by Myra Cohn
Livingston. Reprinted by permission of Marian Reiner for the author.

Liveright Publishing Corporation for "maggie and milly and molly and may,"
from *The Complete Poems, 1913–1962* by e.e. cummings.
Copyright © 1956 by e.e. cummings.
Reprinted with permission of Liveright Publishing Corporation.

Lilian Moore for "Mine" and "Until I Saw the Sea," from *I Feel the Same Way*
by Lilian Moore. Copyright © 1967 by Lilian Moore.
Reprinted by permission of Marian Reiner for the author.

Russell Hoban for "Old Man Ocean," from *The Pedaling Man* by Russell Hoban.
Copyright © 1968 by Russell Hoban.
Reprinted by permission of Harold Ober Associates, Incorporated.

Henry Holt and Company, Inc. / *Publishers since 1866*
115 West 18th Street / New York, New York 10011

Henry Holt is a registered trademark of Henry Holt and Company, Inc.

Compilation copyright © 1995 by Alison Shaw
Photographs copyright © 1995 by Alison Shaw
Design by Sue Dawson
All rights reserved.
Published in Canada by Fitzhenry & Whiteside Ltd.,
195 Allstate Parkway, Markham, Ontario L3R 4T8.

Library of Congress Cataloging-in-Publication Data
Until I saw the sea and other poems / [selected and photographed by] Alison Shaw.
1. Sea poetry, American. 2. Children's poetry, American. 3. Children's poetry, English. 4.
Sea poetry, English. [1. Sea poetry. 2. American poetry. 3. English poetry.]
I. Shaw, Alison.
PS595.S39U58   1995   811.008"032162—dc20   94-28810

ISBN 0-8050-2755-6 / First Edition — 1995
Printed in the United States of America on acid-free paper. ∞

1 3 5 7 9 10 8 6 4 2

Contents

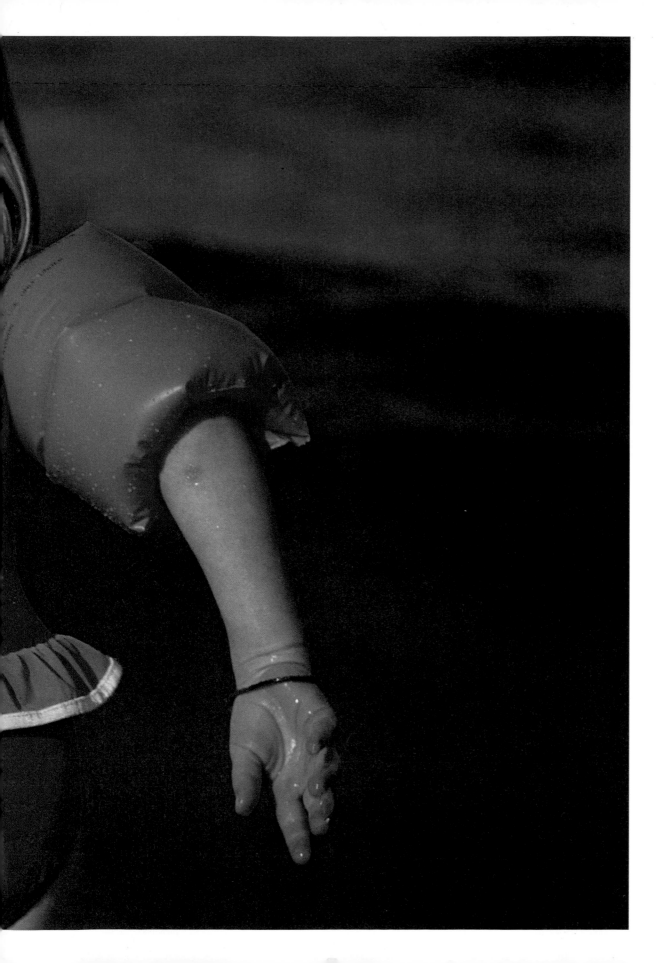

Driving to the Beach

On the road
smell fumes and tar
through the windows
of the car.

But at the beach
smell suntan lotion
and wind
and sun
and ocean!

— JOANNA COLE

Sitting in the Sand

Sitting in the sand and the sea comes up
So you put your hands together
And you use them like a cup
And you dip them in the water
With a scooping kind of motion
And before the sea goes out again
You have a sip of ocean.

— KARLA KUSKIN

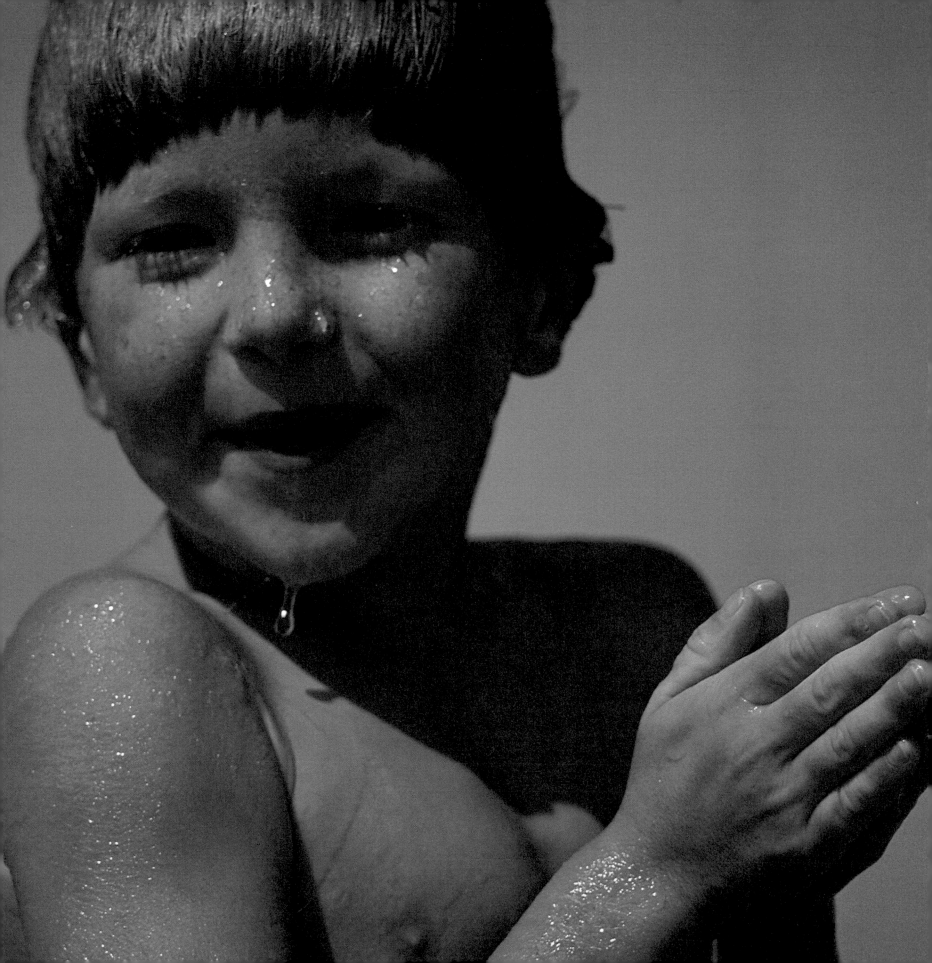

How to Swim

First one ankle, then another,
Then it's time to splash your brother.
Get him good — a sneak attack —
And dive before he splashes back.

Beneath the water, like a crab,
Give your sister's foot a grab.
Giggle bubbles as she screams;
She's not as grown-up as she seems.

Your father warns you to behave,
So ride a giant tidal wave.
It knocks you over — what a beaut! —
And almost steals your bathing suit.

Leave the ocean with a howl.
Mom surrounds you with a towel.
With puckered hands and purple lips,
You're starving for potato chips.

— D.A.W.

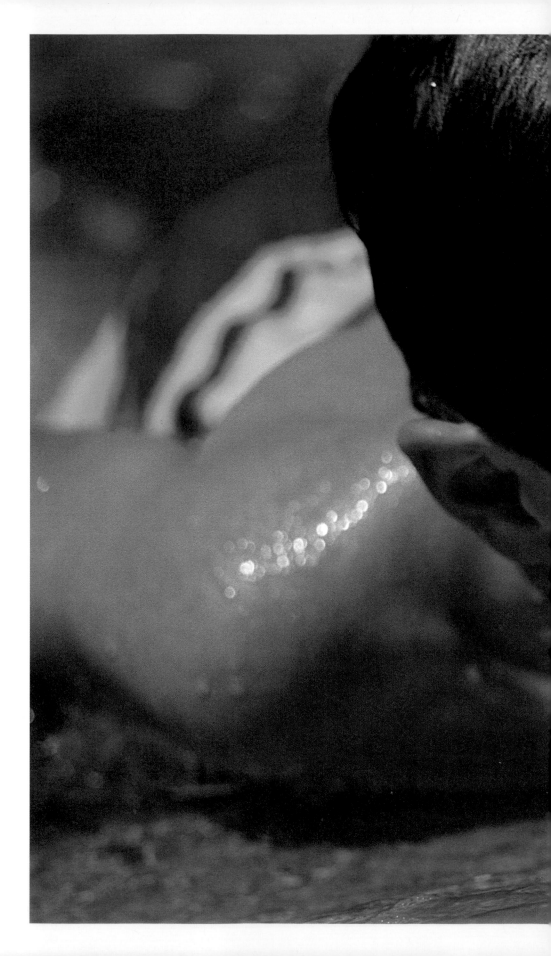

Seashore Recipe

To bake
A seashore cake
Take:
A pail of sand
Sift it, lift it, fill it —
Don't spill it!
Add:
Fresh seawater
A pinch of shore
The ocean's roar
A purple stone
One small whalebone
Two clams
Three red claws
And (if you can find them)
Old fish jaws.
Mix well.
Pour into a lined conch shell.
Set in the sun to bake.
Then presto —
Seashore cake!

— NOLA BUCK

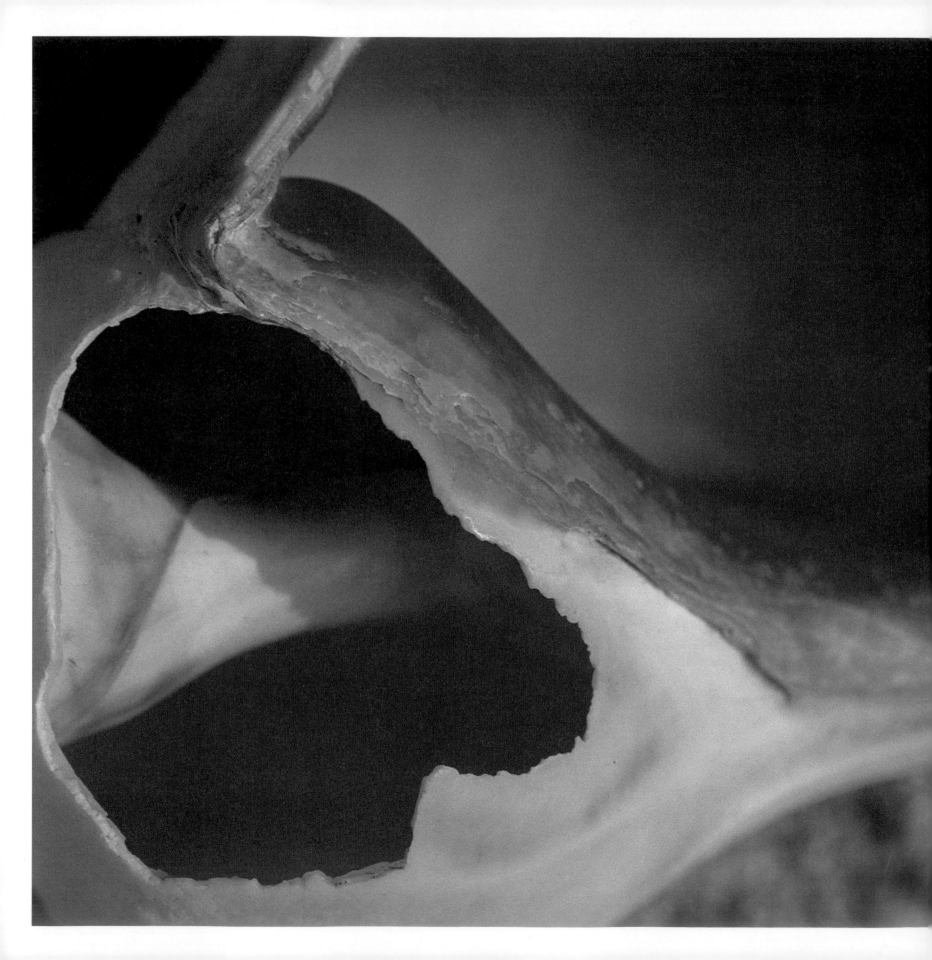

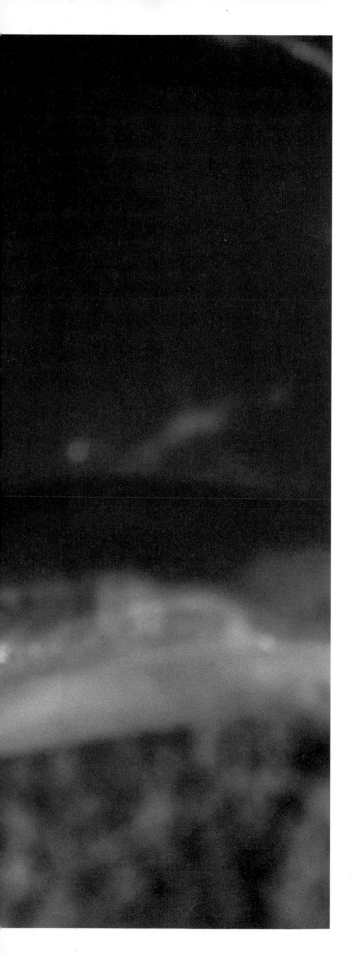

The Shell

I took away the ocean once,
Spiraled in a shell,
And happily for months and months
I heard it very well.

How is it then that I should hear
What months and months before
Had blown upon me sad and clear,
Down by the grainy shore?

— DAVID McCORD

Seaweed

Seaweed from high tide
where sand and breakers meet
gummy
on my tummy,
slippery
on my feet.

— MYRA COHN LIVINGSTON

13

At the Seaside

When I was down beside the sea,
A wooden spade they gave to me
To dig the sandy shore.

My holes were hollow like a cup,
In every hole the sea came up,
Till it could hold no more.

— ROBERT LOUIS STEVENSON

"maggie and milly and molly and may"

maggie and milly and molly and may
went down to the beach (to play one day)

and maggie discovered a shell that sang
so sweetly she couldn't remember her troubles, and

milly befriended a stranded star
whose rays five languid fingers were;

and molly was chased by a horrible thing
which raced sideways while blowing bubbles: and

may came home with a smooth round stone
as small as a world and as large as alone.

For whatever we lose (like a you or a me)
it's always ourselves we find in the sea

— e.e. cummings

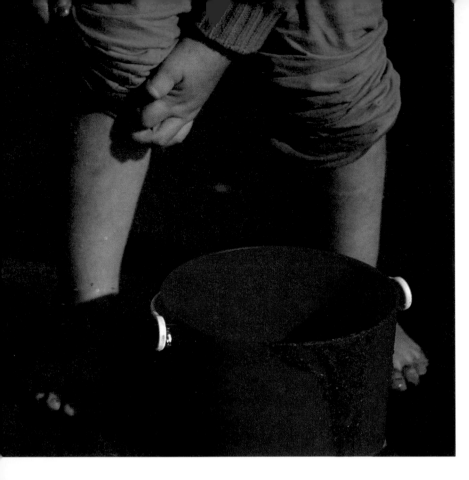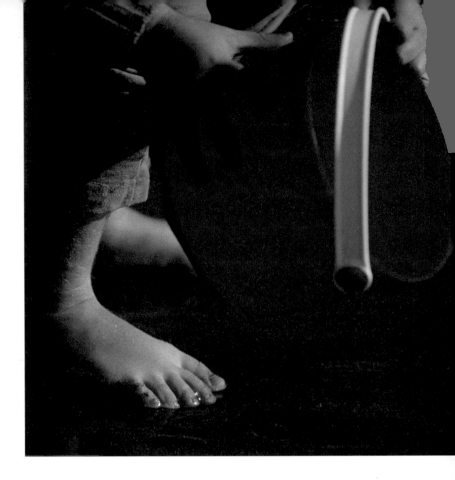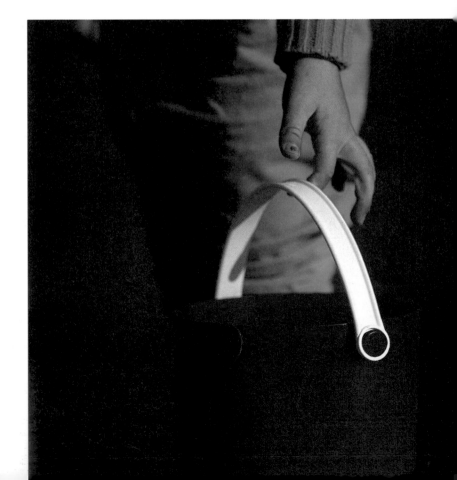

Mine

I made a sand castle.
In rolled the sea.
  "All sand castles
  belong to me —
   to me,"
said the sea.

I dug sand tunnels.
In flowed the sea.
  "All sand tunnels
  belong to me —
   to me,"
said the sea.

I saw my sand pail floating free.
I ran and snatched it from the sea.
  "My sand pail
  belongs to me —
   to ME!"

— LILIAN MOORE

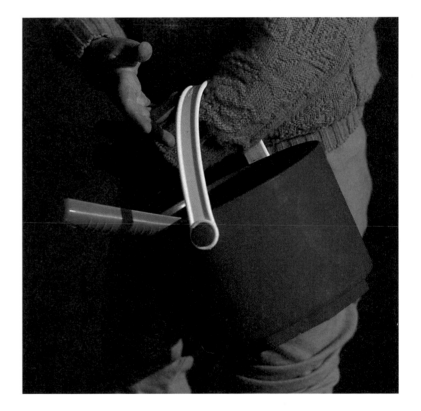

Until
I Saw
the Sea

Until I saw the sea
I did not know
that wind
could wrinkle water so.

I never knew
that sun
could splinter a whole sea of blue.

Nor
did I know before,
a sea breathes in and out
upon a shore.

— LILIAN MOORE

Ferry Me Across the Water

"Ferry me across the water,
   Do, boatman, do."
"If you've a penny in your purse
   I'll ferry you."

"I have a penny in my purse,
   And my eyes are blue;
So ferry me across the water,
   Do, boatman, do!"

"Step into my ferry-boat,
   Be they black or blue,
And for the penny in your purse
   I'll ferry you."

— CHRISTINA ROSSETTI

A Kite

I often sit and wish that I
Could be a kite up in the sky,
And ride upon the breeze and go
Whichever way I chanced to blow.

— ANONYMOUS

One, two, three, four, five,
Once I caught a fish alive,
Six, seven, eight, nine, ten,
Then I let it go again.
Why did you let it go?
Because it bit my finger so.
Which finger did it bite?
The little finger on the right.

— TRADITIONAL

Golden
Fishes

When I was a little boy,
I washed my mammy's dishes;
I put my finger in my eye,
And pulled out golden fishes.

— Anonymous

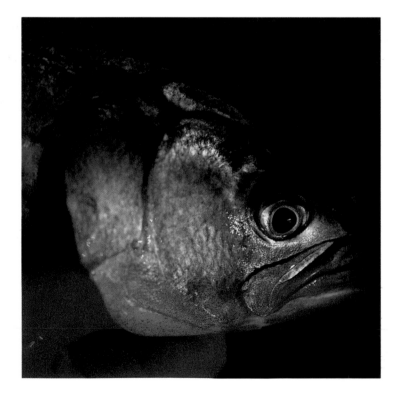

Prayer

"Lord! Let me catch a fish
So large that even I,
In telling of it afterwards,
Shall have no need to lie."

— Anonymous

Old Man
Ocean

Old Man Ocean, how do you pound
Smooth glass, rough stones round?
Time and the tide and the wild waves rolling
Night and the wind and the long gray dawn.

Old Man Ocean, what do you tell,
What do you sing in the empty shell?
Fog and the storm and the long bell tolling,
Bones in the deep and the brave men gone.

— RUSSELL HOBAN

The Sounding Fog

The fog comes in with a big sound
Made of small sounds from all around;

I hear the beat of sea-gulls' wings —
The storm wind as it sighs and sings —

I hear the clanging buoy bell
And dangers that the fog-horns tell.

And every farthest sound of waves
Fog gathers — and it brings — and it saves.

The gray fog hides away the Sea
Then brings it in a roar to me.

— Susan Nichols Pulsifer

29

Sea
Fever

I must go down to the seas again, to the lonely sea and the sky,
And all I ask is a tall ship and a star to steer her by;
And the wheel's kick and the wind's song and the white sail's shaking,
And the gray mist on the sea's face, and a gray dawn breaking.

I must go down to the seas again, for the call of the running tide
Is a wild call and a clear call that may not be denied;
And all I ask is a windy day with the white clouds flying,
And the flung spray and the blown spume, and the seagulls crying.

I must go down to the seas again, to the vagrant gypsy life,
To the gull's way and the whale's way where the wind's like a whetted knife;
And all I ask is a merry yarn from a laughing fellow-rover,
And a quiet sleep and a sweet dream when the long trick's over.

— JOHN MASEFIELD

Nantucket Lullaby

Hush, the waves are rolling in,
    White with foam, white with foam,
Father toils amid the din,
    While baby sleeps at home.

Hush, the ship rides in the gale,
    Where they roam, where they roam,
Father seeks the roving whale,
    While baby sleeps at home.

Hush, the wind sweeps o'er the deep,
    All alone, all alone,
Mother now the watch will keep,
    Till father's ship comes home.

— Anonymous